Dog Cartoons

Coloring Book

Poodle

By Anita Valle

Affenpinscher

Airedale

Akita

Australian Shepherd

Basset Hound

Beagle

Bearded collie

Border collie

Boston Terrier

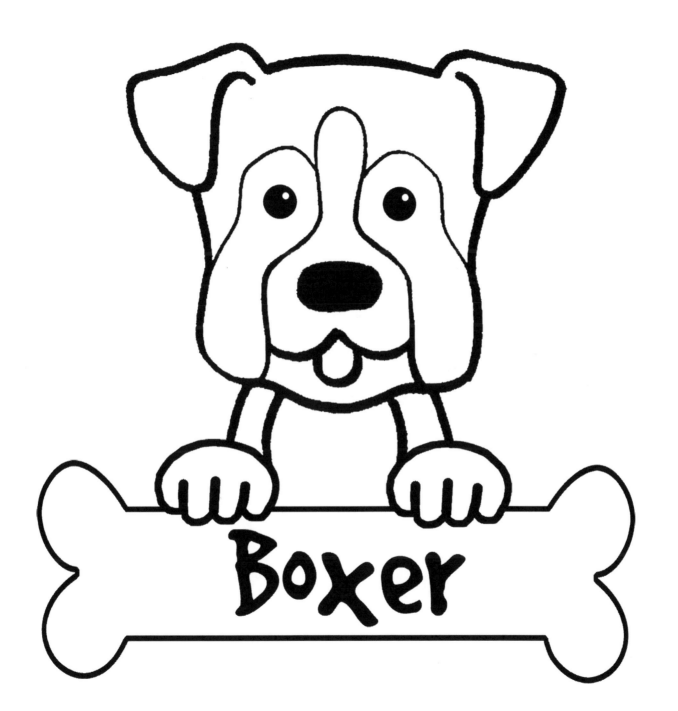

Bull Terrier

Chinese Crested

Chinese Shar-Pei

Chow Chow

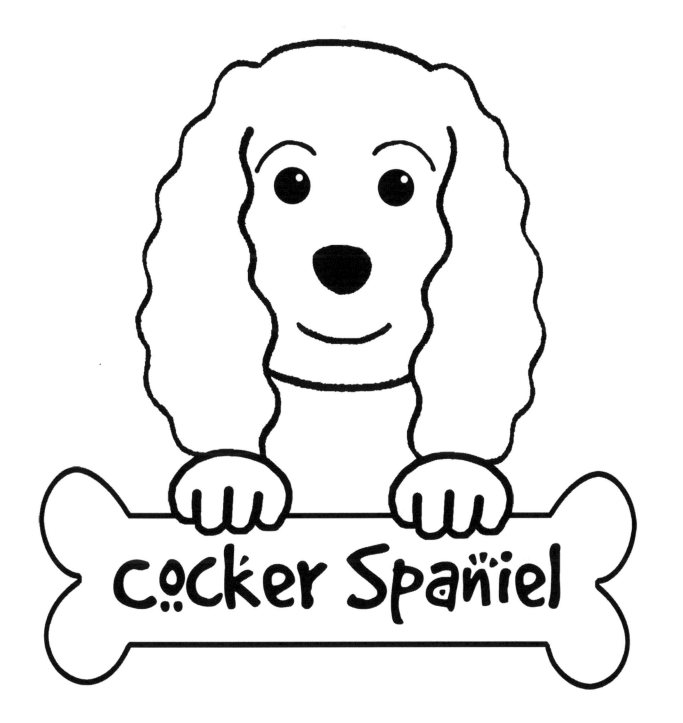

Dalmation

Dandie Dinmont Terrier

Doberman Pinscher

English Foxhound

German Shepherd

Golden Retriever

Lhasa Apso

Miniature Pinscher

Miniature Schnäuzer

Pit Bull

Saint Bernard

1
2
3
4
5
6
7
8
9
10
0

Stella

Scottish Terrier

Every dog featured in this coloring book can be purchased on t-shirts, mugs, tote bags, magnets, stickers, and more! Go to www.zazzle.com/dogcartoons to shop for your favorite dog breed! Over 100 dog breeds available!